Copyright ©
Tiny Owl Publishing 2018

For my dear Amin

Illustrations ©
Nazli Tahvili 2018

First published in the
UK in 2018 by
Tiny Owl Publishing,
London
www.tinyowl.co.uk

ISBN 978-1-910328-32-3

A catalogue record for this book is available from the British Library.

Printed in China

CHALK
EAGLE

NAZLI TAHVILI

TINY OWL

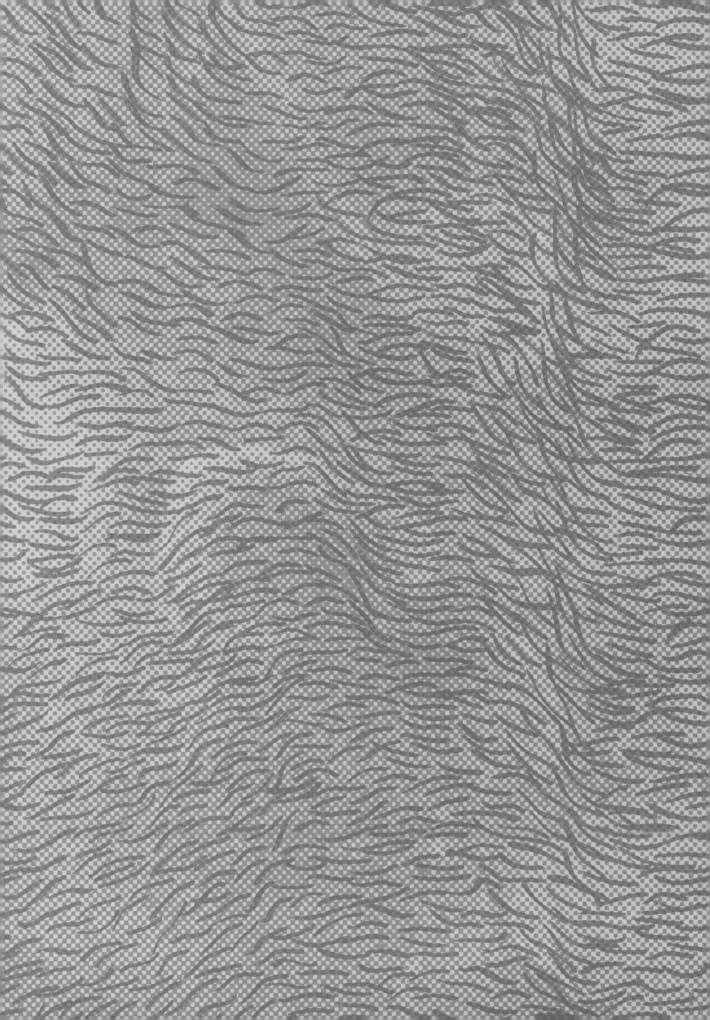

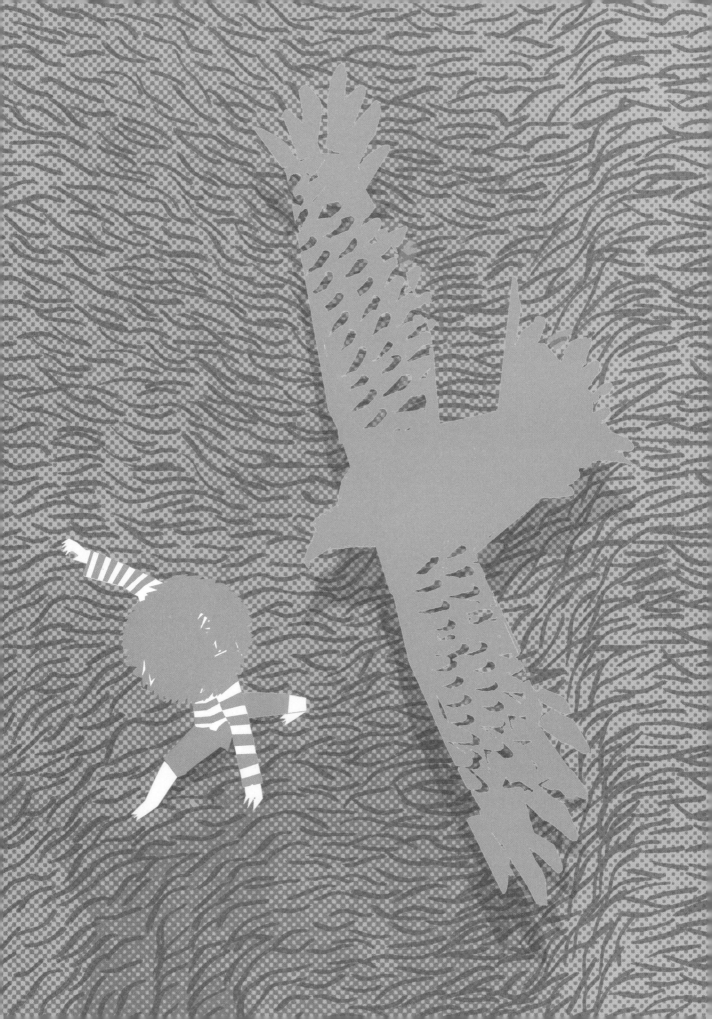

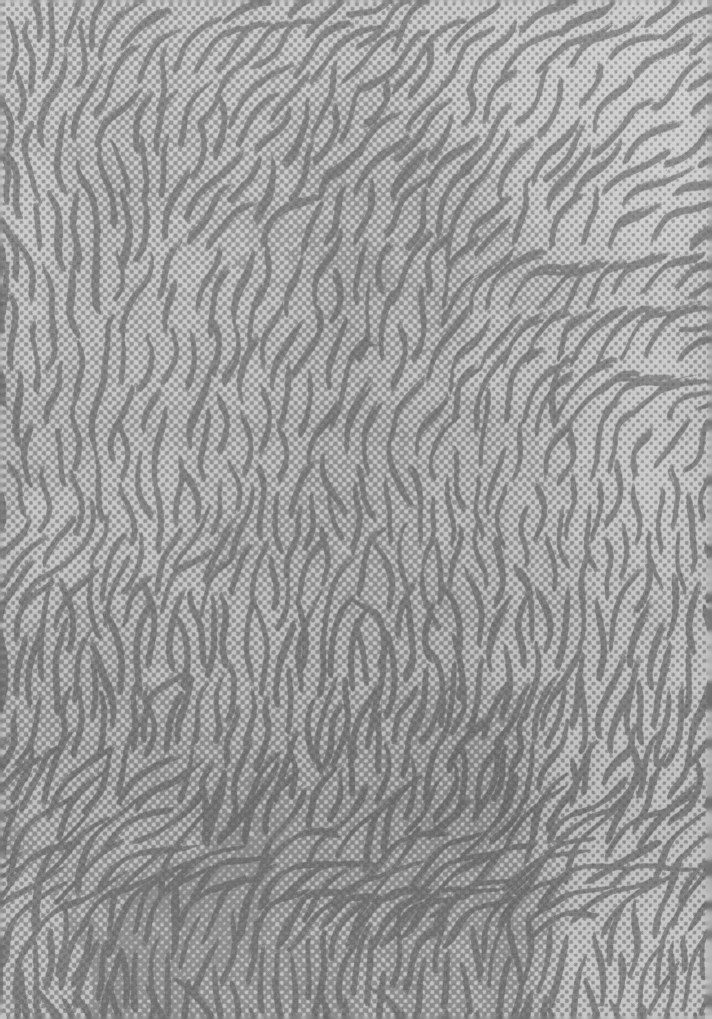

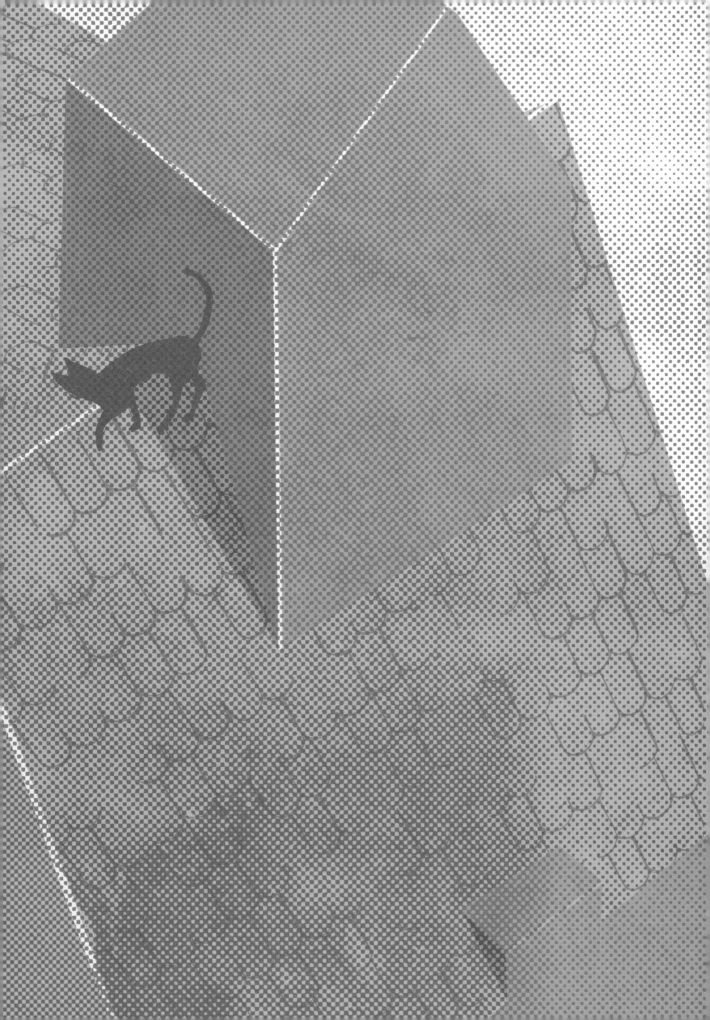

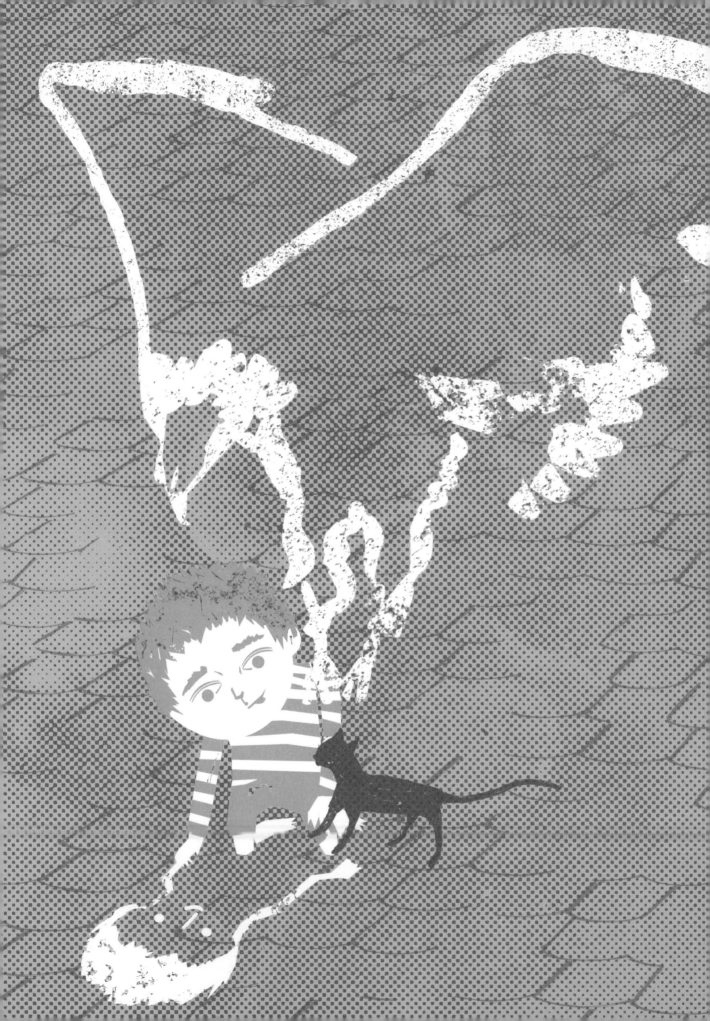

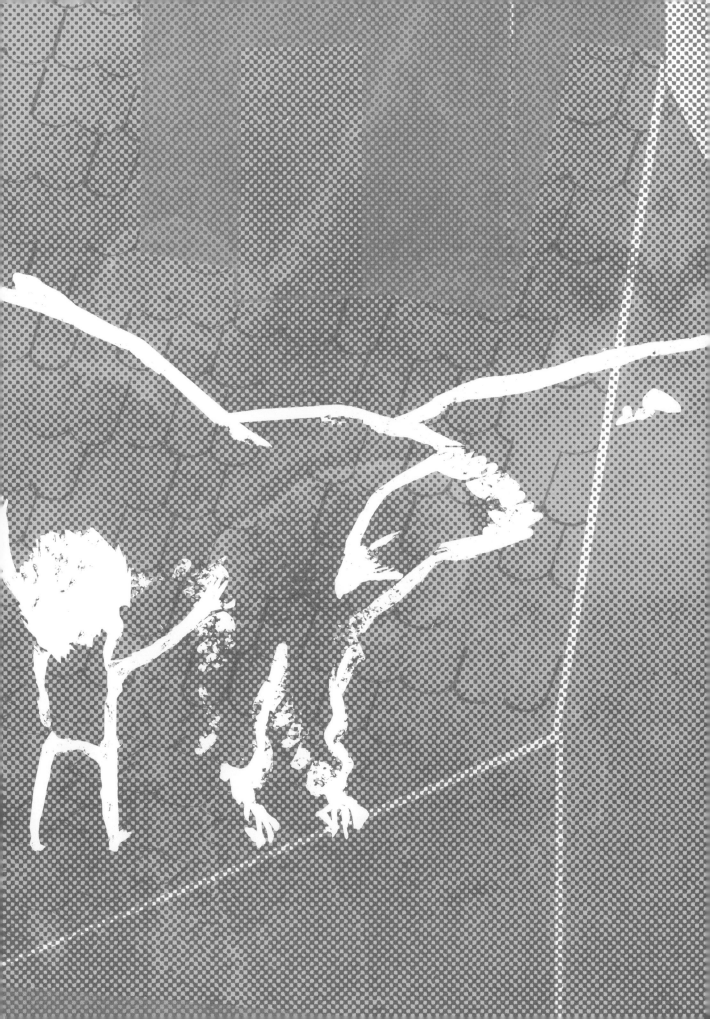

ABOUT NAZLI TAHVILI

The story of Chalk Eagle is based on a memory of my husband's childhood. His name is Amin and he loves birds and horses. When he was a child, Amin often drew with chalk on the rooftop of his house. His favourite drawing was a big eagle. He would draw the eagle and look at it from the window of his small room on the roof. Or he would lie on it and spread his arms like the eagle's wings, and fall asleep with the dream of flying.

Our home and studio is in the north of Iran, surrounded by beautiful rice fields. In the summer, the green of the rice fields, the blue of the sky and the birds flying were the only things you could see. At that time, I was sketching the story of Chalk Eagle, and was affected by the colours of the magnificent, clear greens and blues of my environment, and chose them to create the silkscreen illustrations for my new book.

. . . .

Nazli Tahvili is an award-winning illustrator from Iran. Nazli studied Art and Architecture at Azad University in Tehran, Iran, and at the Academy of Fine Arts in Bologna, Italy.

For more on wordless picture books, visit www.tinyowl.co.uk.